Spunk and Spice

VOLUME 1

B. A. PAUL

Contents

Foreword

I had a decent direction for this foreword with five lines done when a text from my aunt caused me to erase and start again.

On the day I compose this, my grandmother Della has been gone from this world for twenty-nine years. My aunt was a bit sad. Then I got a bit sad. I didn't have as much time with this paternal grandparent as I did my maternal one who lived until the ripe old age of ninety-one.

Grandma Della battled cancer and passed when I was fifteen. And fifteen-year-olds are generally self-absorbed and clueless. They don't ask the correct questions of their elders. They don't value the time and traditions as they should. Fifteen-year-olds believe those "old folks" will be around, well, eternally.

Fast-forward a few decades and this writing thing is dusting off memories long buried and now highly cherished.

Grandma Della loved petunias and flower pots and gardening. I remember her house smelling of vinegar from giant galvanized tubs of cucumbers soaking, destined to become sweet pickles crammed into Mason jars. I remember yellow, sticky messes as we shaved sweet corn off the cobs and packaged the garden glories into freezer bags.

We'd have a contest every spring to see who saw the first butterfly, robin, or rainbow. She'd let me win and I'd get a dollar for my "finds."

She took me to auctions and flea markets and taught me how to cross-stitch and to enjoy the Statler Brothers and John Denver. She was madly in love with Boston Terriers and had a herd of them over the years.

She was full of life and vim and vigor. Of spunk and spice. And it's to Grandma Della that I dedicate this collection of shorts featuring characters, well, full of the same.

Happy reading!

B. A. Paul

The Interruption

Tragedy changes plans and dreams and family dynamics in a hurry. Sometimes for the worse. But sometimes glorious little interruptions can mend the soul.

Rain pats the wood-framed window in the small dining nook, the drops frolicking and blending down the glass in lazy streams. The view of the side yard, the yellows and browns and fiery reds blur and distort as the unexpected shower trumps the autumn rays.

Eugene smiles. An interruption is imminent.

It had taken him many months to appreciate the rain as he had in the "before" days. Before tragedy. Before the massive adjustment no elderly couple should endure. Raindrops were teardrops. Raindrops and their icy counterparts were building blocks of nightmares and anguish.

Until recently.

He rests his hands on the keys of his typewriter—his son wanted him to upgrade, but Eugene was old-school and refused to move the old Royal from its place near the dining nook window. Edith had quilted a pad to go under it to protect the table's finish. His daughter-in-law, savvy shopper, had kept him in grand supply of ribbon cartridges.

A pang ran under his ribs and squeezed the muscles in his chest. The pangs come less often, but when they do, they're no less sharp. His supply of cartridges would run out. He'd have to adjust. Or source the ribbon himself.

How silly of him. Worrying about that.

The door slams. She's almost made her way to the dining nook.

A soft mew escapes the basket under the table. The kitten knows, too, it's time to wake from the midday slumber and greet the princess. But the kitten is young and the urge to sleep in the dish-towel lined basket near the author's feet overtakes the urge to escape the basket. For now.

Eugene shifts his weight in the oak chair and feels his overalls buttons scraping the finish as he pounds out a few more words. Just a few more before the interruption.

Edith used to cringe and fuss over that marring of her dear dining set—from the buttons on his pants to the worn rubber toes of the typewriter. And before that—decades before that—his son's toy tractors and ball and jacks.

Edith had also fussed and cringed over animals in the house. But someone's brown eyes and long lashes changed her mind and she'd buttoned her lip. Mostly.

Today Edith has better things to worry about. She bangs pots and pans and talks to herself in the kitchen, readying the afternoon snack of still-warm snickerdoodles onto three small plates and pouring apple cider spiced with cinnamon sticks into two coffee mugs and one tiny teacup.

The keys clunk and click as he pounds out his manuscript, just a few more lines…

A tiny child runs to the author and presents him a dripping bouquet of fall. She asks for—demands, actually—lap time. So the child can plunk and plink at the keys.

Edith wasn't quite ready with the snack yet. Eugene grins at the tot and adjusts the chair so both can slide their legs under the table. His feet on the floor. Hers swinging freely. The commotion rouses the kitten, who bats at her feet and tries to climb his pants leg.

He rolls the current page of his manuscript—a manuscript only half finished—out of the black Royal and lays it aside. He feeds a fresh, crisp sheet into the machine.

She wiggles in his lap, legs dangling against his shins. He smells her hair, slightly damp from the rain, but the warmth of the afternoon sun in her brunette locks hasn't faded from her outdoor adventures.

His son at this age, once his engineering-bent brain figured out how the typewriter worked, had lost interest in the keys and lap time. He was off building castles and forts and shingling them with layers of foliage not unlike those dripping rainwater onto the table now.

When his son had shown interest again, for an English paper, Eugene had been too busy with too many deadlines to slide from his perch and let the kid take over the keys. Even for an afternoon.

It had been raining that day, too.

Eugene blinks the memory into a far corner. He'd visit there later and try to linger on the young boy with the toy tractors. Not the teenager he'd pushed aside.

Right now, this girl was front and center.

She pushes and fumbles with the keys, her tiny fingers barely strong enough to hold them down for the hammer to make an imprint. The author shows her tricks with the shift button, unlocking a whole secret code.

The space key brings a smile, and the girl watches the roller move the paper several inches before she tires of its function. She prods along as nonsensical black marks appear on the paper. He takes her hand and pushes it against the return lever, sweeping the carriage to the starting position.

Edith comes from the kitchen and sets the cookies and cider on the table, but the grandchild has no interest in snacks at the moment, which slightly irritates Edith, but she recovers and watches the pair as they play with the typewriter. From the corner of his eye, Eugene sees his beautiful wife, beaten and battered from the years of putting up with his reclusiveness. His grumps and groans of aging.

Then the searing agony of loss.

But today, in this instant, Edith casts a rare smile.

Eugene glances up, winks at her, then turns his attention to the Royal.

The author shows the little girl which letters to push to make her name. She grins when he winds the paper up so she can inspect what she's created. CHERISH. All in capitals, as she'd had him hold the shift button down. "All the way Gampaw."

He winds the paper down again. Swipes the return bar.

Reset.

"Kitty's name next, Gampaw."

Twice she pushes too many keys at once and the hammers jumble together above the roller.

Twice he untangles them, squares her on his lap and she starts again.

The child insists on showing the kitten its name on the paper. "I did this, Lucy, see?" The fuzzball bats at the corner, piercing the edge of the sheet with its tiny claw. "No, no. That's not ladylike, Lucy." She returns to his lap and Eugene reinserts the sheet. The kitten, unhappy at being abandoned for a typewriter, saunters off to the living room to perch on the back of the sofa. A better vantage point than under the table.

Eugene shows his granddaughter which letters to push once more. Letters to create a *whole entire sentence.*

She does so, and every time she pushes the correct key, he tickles her ribs, causing her to bend away from his fingers with delightful squeals, kicking him in the shins one second, nearly falling onto the floor the next. Edith, still smiling, issues a warning. Because she's a mom at heart. Because it's her job. Someone's gonna end up bruised…

But he doesn't mind. He squares her again and again on his lap.

Reset. Reset. Reset.

Energy and life radiated like the autumn rays from Cherish. Many times, Edith had wondered if they could handle her. She so young, Edith and Eugene pushing seventy. An entire life in front of her, and the old couple may not live long enough to see the child into middle school. Panic tied them in knots, especially in those early weeks and months after the crash.

The crash where the raindrops had turned into those icy counterparts. A slick turn on a dark country road…

Again, Eugene squares his granddaughter on his lap as he pushes aside the weight of the past. He looks at his wife. Still smiling. Fussing with the cookies. Dabbing up drops of splashed-out cider from the mugs from the jiggling at the table. If the session didn't end soon, more cider would be on Edith's apron than in the cups.

She dabs a tear after dabbing the cider. The corners of her aprons had soaked up her weight in sorrow over the past year. He kisses the child's head again and refocuses.

After the last letter of the sentence, he points to a key, and she slams the period onto the page with flare. He rolls the paper up and shows her the masterpiece. He reads the sentence she so confidently typed under his direction. She giggles and slides from his lap. "I wuv you too, Gampaw."

She races to the sofa and shows Lucy what she's created. A tiny finger runs under the black print. She reads to the kitten a masterful story of kings and queens and princesses named Cherish and Lucy, all while waving the page in the kitten's face.

Lucy bats at the page again, tearing a small corner free. Cherish starts to panic and scold the cat. Edith intervenes and ushers the child back to the nook, takes the paper from the girl and hands it to Eugene.

Edith places the tot in her own chair on top of a stack of Readers Digest hardbacks. The little girl gobbles the cookie and slurps the cider from the teacup as Edith tries to teach her how to be dainty about it. Lady-like.

"Like a princess, Gammaw?"

"Yes, Cherish. Like a princess."

Eugene smiles as he watches his wife and granddaughter. He nibbles and sips at Edith's masterpieces with one wrinkled hand and holds the child's work in the other. Her name is nestled between strings of nonsense—nonsense to him, but fantastic worlds of fairies and knights to Cherish.

The "I Love You." stares at him from the bottom. Near where Lucy took out the chunk.

He runs his thumb over the phrase and feels the indent that final period left in the paper. The trio finishes off the rest of the cookies and cider. Edith wipes down the child's face and hands with her apron— those poor aprons—and scoots her off the booster pile of books. One book topples to the floor. Cherish scoops it up and rushes away to read to Lucy again.

He glances through the door where the child plays with the calico kitten in the next room. All bubbly giggles as the kitten chases her energetic feet across the braided rug. A string of nonsense coming from Cherish's lips as she "reads" one flipped page after another.

Edith cleans up the table then joins Cherish and Lucy. She chooses a storybook from the shelf near the sofa. She sits. Cherish drops the Readers Digest with a thud and snuggles next to Gammaw. The kitten follows. The sudden burst of energy dissipates into lazy afternoon still- ness. Cherish lays her head in Edith's lap. Edith strokes her hair as she reads of ladies and knights.

Eugene watches the only two who matter now. He wished he'd understood what mattered in the lifetime before this one. When the busyness of life pushed aside moments like these for "after while," "later," or "tomorrow."

That brown-eyed little boy of his didn't wait for the after whiles, laters or tomorrows. This brown-eyed little girl wouldn't wait, either.

But Eugene had learned. Take the interruptions as they come. Edith had learned there's more important worries than blemishes on the old oak dining set.

The rain continues its tap dance against the window in the dining nook. Drops blend to create new streams. Unpredictable in their twists and turns.

Cherish napped on the sofa, the cat by her feet. Edith dozed sitting straight up. Eugene didn't worry about waking them. The tap dance of the Royal's keys was like background music in their tiny home.

The interruption is over too soon. These interruptions always are.

He gathers the still-damp leaves and the child's paper and sets them to the side of the typewriter next to the loose manuscript pages.

The dedication page, his visual anchor, rests on the top of the pile.

He rubs his wrinkled hands together, massaging out the soreness from the wrestle with Cherish. He reloads the manuscript page into the machine as he reads the two-line dedication—a ritual he performs each time he loads a new page.

> *In memory of my loving son and his wonderful wife.*
> *And to Cherish, forever.*

A single, humble tear escapes down his cheek. He lets it go. He takes a deep breath and starts plunking and clinking the keys exactly where he left off before the glorious interruption.

Reset.

Green Thumb

The coveted River Bluff Green Thumb Garden trophy is up for grabs again this year, and Gladys Olson is dead set on winning it as she has done for so many years. But Twila Davis has one of the judges in her pocket and is willing to go way out of bounds to be declared the best. Then again, some things are more important than winning, and Gladys's quest for the trophy may return to her something far more valuable.

Gladys Olson dusted off her hands and knees, took four steps backward, and surveyed her progress. Over the course of the last week and a half, she'd dug sod, laid marbled stepping stones and plotted where she would plant each flower, bush and sprig in her massive compass rose flower bed. She'd mixed in fertilizers with just the right pH for each section's plants.

She was missing one final piece, and she planned to solve that problem shortly.

Last year, Francine, down the block, had won the coveted River Bluff Green Thumb Garden trophy. The Garden Association passed the trophy from gardener to gardener after the mid-summer judging. The three years prior to that, the trophy, a life-sized bronzed gardening glove with a green quartz thumb overlay, had sat on Gladys's mantel. One year for every season that Gladys competed.

Until Francine one-upped her with that ridiculous castle-themed bed complete with gurgling moat and cement knight on horseback. It was the gaudiest thing Gladys had ever seen, but the Association threw Francine a sympathy vote because her husband had just died the previous fall. Gladys's man had passed four years ago, which is how Gladys now found the time to plan and cultivate and dream.

Once upon a time, when their husbands were alive, the couples had spent lots of time together. After Ted died, though, Gladys just didn't want to fool with social niceties.

And this year Gladys would rescue the Green Thumb and return it to its rightful spot above the fireplace.

Gladys grinned.

Then she'd invite Francine over for tea.

She went inside for a quick freshening up, grabbed her wallet and drove the old Lucerne to the estate auction at the edge of town. She slowed in front of Francine's yard to spy on her progress. She was down on hands and knees, planting petunias.

Petunias! The cheapest, easiest flowers on the planet. The Association wouldn't look too kindly on her efforts. Not with petunias.

That meant Gladys might have a chance to win the trophy. She'd be sure to win with the centerpiece for her compass rose without too much competition.

A crowd gathered on the lawn as Gladys parked her car on the street in front of the old house. Mr. and Mrs. Steckson had grown old together, grew ill together, and passed away in the same nursing home room. Together.

Not a bad run. Gladys had thought maybe she and Ted would do the same. The cancer had had other ideas, though.

The Steckson children wanted nothing to do with the family home. They'd grown up and had left River Bluff, population nine hundred forty-two, for a more lucrative life in the big city. They'd hired some big-shot auctioneers to man the estate sale, and the kids, now grown with kids of their own, hadn't even bothered to show up.

Gladys checked in with the auctioneer at a small folding table on the front lawn. She paid three dollars for a paddle to bid with, paddle number 213, and joined the crowd. She hoped most of them were here for the house or vehicles, and not the single item Gladys had in mind.

The one thing she was determined not to leave the premises without.

The auction started with the big-ticket items. House, car, appliances. Then the auctioneer opened the gate and directed the crowd, now thinned out by half, to look through the items which had been boxed, organized and tagged in the back yard.

Gladys could hardly believe what she saw. The Stecksons' back yard looked barren. If River Bluff had had rain in the last few days, the entire yard would have been a muddy mess.

The old couple had been in the nursing home, but not for that long. Maybe the kids did something to it so they wouldn't have to fiddle with mowing. Or pay someone else to take care of it.

In the corner by the fence, covered in dead brown ivy, was the statue that Gladys envisioned as the centerpiece for her award-winning flower bed. Mrs. Steckson had talked her husband into buying it for her on their vacation to Cape Cod—the only trip he ever took her on. Gladys had been in love with the creature from first sight.

Made in sections of solid concrete, the sea monster appeared to float. The three back sections arched up in half circles, spikes reaching for the sky, and its head faced straight out, mouth open with forked tongue to match the forked tail.

The expression on its face was almost human, and Gladys had teased Ted years ago that the dragon looked a lot like him after losing one of their bridge games with the Stecksons. "Well, when I'm dead, maybe you could marry it."

Gladys smiled at the memory. Right now, the dragon floated on barren dust with dead eyes. But in Gladys's garden, the creature would float in and out of a sea of blue morning glories at the center of the flower bed. And she planned on cleaning and scrubbing the dead moss and lichens from it, and from the green inset eyes until they shone bright again.

"Got your eye on the serpent, huh, Gladys?"

She jumped. It was Andy Trevmore, the Garden Association's head.

"Andy," she squeaked. She hadn't spoken much all morning and she had to clear her throat. It made her sound spooked, and she hated that, especially in front of the Garden Association President. "What brings you here?" She avoided his question.

"Looks like the exact thing that brings you, Mrs. Olson."

Her shoulders sank. Andy was ruthless and dirty and always got what he wanted, no matter who he hurt in the process. Like the head chair of the Garden Association.

Like other men's wives.

Rumor had it he was sweet on Twila Davis. The one-year widowed lady who'd won the Green Thumb every year before Gladys started competing. Rumor also had it he had been sweet on Twila while her husband was still kicking.

Ted and Gladys had teased each other often about whether the surviving spouse would remarry. Ted told her Andy would be happy to have her. Gladys would always jab him in the ribs and say, "Over my stone-cold dead body."

Andy twirled his paddle on the palm of his hand and gave her a sly wink. She wanted to smack him on the back of the head with paddle number 213, but she refrained. She may need his vote in a couple of months.

The auctioneer started the bidding on the random boxes of household items near the back porch. The sea serpent likely would be last.

An hour passed, and Gladys began to feel the noonday sun beating on the back of her neck. She started to fan herself with the paddle, but caught her action just in time, lest she bid with money she didn't have on a box of junk she didn't want.

Four bidders remained when the dragon came up for bid. "Here, we have the Loch Ness Monster, as we call him in the big city."

Gladys and the others moaned. The pompous city auctioneer was getting on the wee town folk's nerves.

"We'll start at twenty."

Gladys waved her paddle. So did the other three.

"Thirty." Everyone bid.

"Fifty." One dropped out. Gladys was on a budget. She knew the Stecksons paid several hundred dollars for the statue, but she had no idea of its value today.

"One hundred." Gladys and Andy waved their paddles. The other bidder dropped out. It was a race to the finish. After each increment, he'd shoot her that ridiculous wink.

At two hundred, Gladys felt the nerves get to her and nearly dropped her paddle because her palms were so sweaty. She almost asked Andy if he'd just drop out. If this went much longer, she'd be into next year's budget for the garden competition. Out of nowhere, or out of stupidity, she held her paddle high and with force yelled "Four hundred dollars!"

The auctioneer took a step back, as did Andy.

"Well, then. Four hundred, going once," he looked straight at Andy, the only one left, "going twice. Sold!"

Andy, too shocked to bid, stood there with his mouth hanging open. Gladys gave him an evil wink and went to the table to pay for her prize.

The auctioneer and his team helped her load the pieces of the statue into her trunk. Andy met her at the car. "That was quite sneaky, Miss

Gladys. I had grand plans for this, but I sure hope you enjoy him." He reached out and rubbed the serpent's face, scrubbing some of the scum off the gemstone eye.

"Thanks. I will. Have a nice day." Gladys reached up to shut the trunk, and Andy yanked his hand back.

She grinned all the way home. "Well, Ted. Looks like I found me another man after all! A stone-cold man!"

For weeks, Gladys planted and tended her compass rose garden. The sea serpent swam among the blue morning glories, just as she'd planned. The judging always took place in the mornings, so she positioned the dragon's head eastward. Each section of the compass was framed by the blue morning glories, and rivers of the blue blossoms flowed from the serpent's pool in the middle. The other sections held shades of yellows and whites, to mimic the rising sun.

Gladys was so impressed with her masterpiece, that she'd get up just before dawn to watch the sun glint off the dragon's eyes. After all the scrubbing it had taken to clean him up, the eyes were the most amazing.

Every few days, Francine would walk past Gladys's yard. Sometimes she'd stop Gladys for a chat. Francine told her how she missed playing cards when their husbands were alive. And the Stecksons. And she was glad that Gladys gave the serpent a good home. Francine had wanted to attend the auction herself, but her funds were low.

Slowly, over those early summer days, Gladys realized Francine was in a true bind. The faintest edges of guilt wiggled their way into the back of her mind over being so competitive. Then she thought about the trophy and pushed them aside, determined to stay focused until judging day.

"You know, you and Twila are the only ones truly in the running this year, right?" Francine called to Gladys one morning.

"Oh, I don't know about that." Gladys wasn't sure how to answer. "I think you're doing just fine."

Francine grinned. "I'm only doing it because Ed encouraged me to participate before he passed. He even went to auctions and flea markets with me the year prior to gather supplies for my castle and moat. His idea, not mine."

Gladys's guilt seared her pride. "I had no idea, Francine. It really was marvelous."

Francine nodded. "Andy gave me the vote because Ed was gone and he was, well, being Andy. You should have won that year, too."

Gladys put down her watering can and joined Francine on the sidewalk. "You mean to tell me Andy came on to you?"

"Not just came on. Outright blatant, he was. I think I got the trophy because Andy is a filthy old man."

Gladys wondered back to the first year she won the trophy. The year after Ted had died. It couldn't have been. Andy didn't say anything directly to her, but maybe.

No. Her garden had been the best that year, and the two following. Or had it?

Her mind raced through every interaction with Andy she could remember. She never liked the way she felt around him, but she hadn't noticed anything—oh dear goodness. Maybe…

"Francine, I think Andy may have awarded me that—"

"Oh, don't go there. I shouldn't have brought it up."

"Twila, you say? Have you seen her entry?"

Francine nodded solemnly, then grinned. "You've got this one in the bag, sweetheart."

Gladys felt only a little relieved. She felt more put off. That he could try to bribe widows like that was… well, incomprehensible. She had always treated him coolly. Maybe handing her the trophy every year had been his way of softening her up.

"Well, I'd better get back to it. Judging is in the morning."

"Good luck!"

"Hey, Francine?"

"Yeah?"

"Good luck to you, too." Gladys meant it with all sincerity, and she wasn't referring to the competition.

Francine smiled and went on her way.

Gladys gazed over her garden. It was gorgeous. She took a deep breath. Regardless of motives or trophies or competition, she had enjoyed herself immensely and would probably keep the installation for the following year. She'd pull out of the Green Thumb altogether so long as Andy had anything to do with it.

Gladys went in to freshen up. She had a few odds and ends to do in the next town over and was going to treat herself to a nice Italian meal out.

∼

She arrived home at dusk. The fireflies floated from the grass and from her flower bed. From the flower bed which seemed a little less circular than it had when she'd left a few hours before.

She approached her compass rose garden and fell to her knees. Something had dug up the ocean and rivers of morning glory vines and left them in shredded bits all over the yard.

She scrambled to see if any of them were viable, but most of the tender vines had been out of the ground too long. Others were so badly mangled that she couldn't save any of them.

The dragon didn't float in a sea of blue green. He sat in a barren wasteland much like the one Gladys had rescued him from. Two of his midsections lay on their sides. She bent to set them straight and lost her breath when she saw the sea dragon's face.

She slipped her hands over the sides of his head to his green marble eyes. Her fingertips fell into empty concrete indentations where the magnificent creature's green orbs had been.

"No! No, no, no!" Gladys sat next to the dragon and sobbed. She cried for Ted and for Francine and for the Stecksons. She cried for her garden and for her dragon and for being so silly as to cry about such things as gardens and dragons. And trophies.

She righted herself, cleaned up the mess as well as she could and called it a night. It was too dark to do anything about it now. The judging committee, headed by Andy Trevmore himself, would stand in her yard at daybreak, shaking their heads and making notes on their green clipboards.

She would replant and fix the dragon's eyes somehow. But the competition was over.

Her alarm went off before dawn, and Gladys gave serious thought to staying in bed. But Ted would tell her she was being a wimp. "Face the music and dance," he'd tell her.

She got dressed and went outside, not wanting to face the compass or the committee.

She was greeted by a dozen people or more, pointing and smiling. People had no consideration for—

Then she followed their gaze to her garden. The magnificent dragon floated on a sea of purple and white petunias. The petunia blooms flowed from the sea in the center in all directions of the compass. The yellows and whites and oranges of the contrasting flowers glowed in the morning sun.

As did the cobalt blue gemstones of the dragon's eyes.

Gladys stood with her mouth open. Francine made her way out of the crowd. "Shut your jaw and take the win!" she whispered.

Gladys stared at Francine as she stuffed dirty gardening gloves into her back pocket. Her knees and elbows were covered, as well.

Twila skulked to the back of the group, but Andy caught her by the arm. The couple were clearly in a tiff as the rest of the committee admired the flowerbed. Andy let Twila go and declared Gladys's entry the grand prize winner.

"I already turned in the trophy." Francine nodded toward Andy, who was fumbling with the five-pound bronze glove on its marble base. The lime-green thumb held little appeal to Gladys at that moment. The rekindled friendship with Francine was win enough. Francine gave her a shove toward the center of the yard.

"Ahem. Ladies—ladies and gentlemen," Andy stuttered. Gladys stopped listening to him drone on. It didn't matter anymore.

As Andy handed her the trophy, standing there on the sidewalk in front of her house, he whispered, "I don't know how you did it, but you're an amazing woman."

Gladys's stomach turned as she took the trophy from him.

The crowd drew in closer to applaud.

She cleared her throat. "Thank you. Thank you all for coming. I couldn't have done it alone." She smiled at Francine. "And this is the perfect way to end several great years of competition. I won't be entering again because I can't possibly top this year's flowerbed." She faced a surprised Andy. "So I won't be needing this."

Gladys dropped the trophy on Andy's foot, sending him hopping on one leg backward where he lost his balance and landed hard on his butt in front of everyone.

Every widow in the group cheered. Everyone but Twila.

Gladys left the chaos on the sidewalk and hugged Francine.

Gladys smiled at her and said, "Want to come in for some tea?"

Dressing Dad

When Hayes takes his elderly father on a day pass to a ballpark, he knew the task would prove challenging. The drought and a lack of understanding turn the challenge into an ordeal that will reveal more than Hayes bargained for.

I reach into the back of the tiny closet in room 402 of The Pines Assisted Living Resort and tug on the only piece of luggage my father owns. It's sad, really. Once a world traveler, only the best of high-end cases and carry-ons would suit him. But for the final leg of his journey, we'd kept only this one piece, which is refusing to come into the light of day.

"God didn't make a deal with you, Pop," I say to him. He glares at me from the vinyl-covered recliner where he waits for his aide.

When I was a kid, I'd looked forward to Dad arriving home after one of his business trips. I'd wait out on the sidewalk in the summers or draped over the back of the sofa staring out the picture window during the winters with my red plastic-handled safety scissors in eager anticipation of cutting off the airport luggage tags to add to my scrapbook collection. Places I'd never been to, and likely would never see in my lifetime. Dad would describe these mystical cities in great detail over Mom's standard welcome-home meal of meatloaf, fried potatoes, and homemade applesauce.

In my eight-year-old brain, these were mysterious lands filled with the grandest of dragons and knights and damsels in distress.

But really, they were the destinations my engineer father traveled to "to better the world with sustainable solutions for agriculture and aquatic needs." Whatever that meant. I'm still not entirely clear. By the time I was ten, I'd memorized all the state-side airport codes. LAX, Los Angeles. LGA, LaGuardia in New York City. BNA — my favorite and closest to our rural Tennessee home an hour's drive from Nashville.

My four sisters and I were well cared for, well fed, and possibly even loved, though Mom's gears were permanently stuck in single-motherhood survival mode as Dad was gone forty-eight weeks out of the year and many weekends. Several years in a row he was home long enough to create another child for her to care for.

Maybe he didn't want her to be lonely.

The suitcase topples into the room with us after a tussle with some fallen clothes hangers. No airport tags on this black case. Not many dings on it, either. Every button-up, sweater vest, and tan trousers the old fart owns would easily fit inside. But he won't need all of his outfits for our weekend pass.

"God didn't make a deal with you, Pop," I say again as I toss the case onto his hospital bed and unzip the lid. I reach for a couple of button-ups and a pair of pants that didn't have coffee stains dripping down the leg.

"Yes. We've got a deal. I'll drink when he sends rain. No rain. No drinking."

"So, if you lived in Seattle, you'd be urinating in your pants every third hour from over-hydrating?"

Dad laughs. "You don't understand God."

"You don't understand biology."

Anna walks into the room and hears this exchange. "You know arguing with him won't do any good." She reaches into the closet for his slip-on house shoes and slides them into the mesh lining of the suitcase lid.

"Coddling him, won't either. And this time his health is at risk," I whisper. Anna has been my father's memory aide at The Pines since his admission here four years ago. She's been great. A staple and great source of grounding and orientation for both Dad and me. But this time, she's dead wrong.

"See, Anna understands God."

"Yes, Mr. Tandy. I do. But I don't think he'd mind if you took some juice with your breakfast this morning. Before you leave with Hayes."

"Who's Hayes?"

"I'm Hayes, Dad. Your son."

"I thought you looked familiar. Where's Karen?" He adjusts his red-framed glasses on his nose.

I sink onto the bed. I knew the weekend would be long if he was having a good spell. This newest obsession with fluid restrictions will definitely put a challenging spin on things. "Karen couldn't come. She's got the kids. Your grandkids, Dad."

He smiles. "I knew I'd have grandkids someday."

Anna, always patient, hands Dad a silver-framed photo from the dresser. "Here's Karen. And your grandchildren, see? Do you remember their names?" Dad takes the photo from her and runs his thumb gently over all the faces. My theory is that Karen keeps herself as busy as Mom did popping out kids so as not to deal with anything Dad-related. But it's just a theory.

Dad hands the photo back to Anna, but he doesn't buy into the name-your-relative game.

Doesn't or can't. I can't tell.

I hand him an opened bottle of water and he knocks it from my hand.

"When the man upstairs sends water, I'll drink it."

Anna pulls me aside into the hallway as she pages for house-keeping to mop up the spill. "He just started this late last night. There's no danger yet. If he hasn't drunk anything by tomorrow, he'll weaken and become more confused."

"What got this started? He's never pulled this one before." He'd pulled plenty of other antics, though. Only wearing green on Sundays. Only eating red foods on Fridays. Always keeping a newspaper to read through the day, never TV. We aren't even sure if he can read anymore, but the papers are a must, and when we'd visit him midday, we usually find him sitting in his side chair, legs crossed, paper laid across his lap, his red-framed glasses sliding down to the tip of his nose.

"He'd overheard a visiting family yesterday talk about how bad the drought has gotten. How the crops are suffering. We didn't know he'd been listening. His face lit up, and he started on about irrigation systems and drainage. And how he could fix the aquatic problem."

I moan. "Well, I guess it makes a little bit of sense. He was an irriga-tion engineer at one time." Which had nothing to do with God Almighty—only the genius solutions thought up by the great Franklin Tandy. I'd learned over the years as Dad's dementia worsened that even the most obtuse thought processes can have some tether to reality —albeit coiled and tangled tethers.

"Hayes, there's no rain in the forecast for the next few days. We may need your consent to start IV fluids if he persists in this current whim. Keep a close eye on him. Maybe offer him moisture-heavy foods, watermelon and soups and such. And don't hesitate to take him to the ER. Though that would end with sedation, no doubt."

The last time Dad had a hospitalization for an acute illness, the ER staff had to call in backup personnel to hold him down. Karen, who has no clue what's been going on with Dad, not really, wanted to get a judge involved to deal with the "inhumane" treatment Dad had received, since Karen believed he shouldn't have been hospitalized to begin with. Karen remains clueless regarding all things dementia. If the decision had been up to her, he'd still be living alone in our family home setting fires in the kitchen and walking around the yard naked.

Both of which have happened.

Jen and I got a judge to declare him incompetent shortly thereafter and had power of attorney papers drawn up. We happily left Karen and my other two sisters out of it. Meg and Tonya visit every few months and are happy to have only that simple duty. Karen, drowning in her own four walls' worth of family, would've liked to been involved, but Jen and I can't deal with her drama.

I didn't want another sedation fiasco for him. Hopefully, we could get through the weekend without him dropping from dehydration. "Maybe I should cancel the plans until he's over this." But I think of the nonrefundable money already spent on our outing. Not that he's not worth it—he is—but things can get tight this time of year.

"Maybe a change of scenery will make him forget and he'll get thirsty enough to drink. We've seen similar results in other residents when they go on outings. And I'll label his outfits so there's no fuss."

"Label? What do you mean?"

"He likes to wear certain garments on certain days." Anna follows the housekeeper with mop and bucket into Dad's room. I watch from the doorway as she happily goes about rearranging and tagging the clothing I'd already packed, tucking in socks and underwear as she went.

I'd promised to take him away for the weekend months ago. A father-son trip, now that he was "retired" and had time to enjoy himself. That was how I'd spun it. Looking back, I think I'd planned this trip out of guilt because Jen has dutifully run point and visited Dad for years. Me, not so much. I'm not too comfortable with the caretaking and only visit once a month or so. Maybe to one-up the other three sisters.

I do take care of the black-and-white tasks of dollar bills and paperwork.

I thought maybe this would give Jen a break. Jen, our family's stable emotional cup-filler since Mom passed. I thought it might give Dad a break from the home. Mostly, though I thought it might ease my miserable conscience. Three months ago when I'd presented this option to Dad, I thought he'd look forward to a weekend of baseball and some of his favorite barbecue eateries around Nashville. A weekend away from The Pines to have an adventure.

But our weekend, and my name, is fresh news to the great Franklin Tandy on this dry, hot Thursday morning.

"Would you mind getting me a paper?" Dad settles himself into the corner booth of the diner.

"We don't have any papers, sir. No one bought them anymore, so we cut off our subscription service. I can adjust the TV to the news channel."

"No. Those jokers are all a bunch of liars on the tube. The only true news is printed news."

I can tell he's getting riled up. And we are only twenty minutes into our extended weekend pass. I could throw a rock and hit The Pines' front gate. "Dad, I'll find you a paper later. Right now, Anna wants us to stay on schedule with your mealtimes. What sounds good?" Throwing Anna's name around may carry more weight since he can't remember mine. Or what we're doing. I slide the plastic-coated, single-page menu in front of him. I've no idea how to get his dementia meds down him if he doesn't drink something. I dig out the baggie of noon medication Anna had handed me back at The Pines. Three tiny pills, the names of which I can't pronounce.

All I have to do is get him to take a few sips and three tiny pills…

"Can I get you some coffee or water?" The waitress, holey jeans and baggy tee-shirt, stood at the ready with her little ticket book. I hope she's not in for a show.

"God and I have a deal." He looks up at her over his glasses. "When he sends rain, I'll drink."

Yup. Lunch and a show. This will cost me extra in tips, I can feel it down to my toes. "Do you serve soup?" I ask.

"Vegetable and chili."

"One of each, two glasses of water, and a cup of fruit." I figured the more items on the table, the better chance he'd munch, slurp or sip something without realizing it.

"Could you bring me today's newspaper?" Dad scans the menu and hands it back to our confused waitress who's about to answer him again, but I interrupt.

"It's okay." I try to wink at her, but now I think she must think I'm trying to come on to her. And wouldn't that be something. She's young enough to be my daughter.

"Dad, I'm going to have to take you back to The Pines if you don't take these pills and then we'll miss our baseball game. So when the nice girl comes back with the waters, I need you to cooperate. Please."

"I've never taken pills a day in my life." He crosses his arms over his chest, revealing a tiny hole in the armpit of his pale blue sweater vest, and looks out the window. "But I do like baseball. My son does, too." He stares at a maintenance worker across the street. He follows the man's movements and seems interested in what he's doing.

Examining Dad's profile, I notice the dark age spots dotting his temple and cheek. Faint scuff marks run the length of his eyeglass's ear piece. His jaw is littered with fine gray stubble and his ear hair needs trimmed—something he'd been meticulous about when he was in his prime. The wrinkles at the corner of his eyes are deeper set than I remember from my last visit a couple of months ago. Maybe I simply wasn't paying attention then.

I was only paying my dues.

I follow his gaze out the window, but a dark moving van parking along the sidewalk turns my view of the street into a hazy mirror. I stare at my own profile in the muddled reflection. Crows feet, a faint age spot, and a dotting of my own graying stubble stare back. My stomach knots. Time marches me into my father's well-forged path whether I choose to go or not.

Dad grins at me when the gal brings our food. A grin I can't read. Is he happy? Playful? Ornery?

I hand him a spoon, and he plays with the grapes and melon in the fruit bowl but doesn't eat anything.

"Dad, no baseball if you don't take—"

"Fine!" He puts the pills in his mouth dry. Chews twice. His eyes tear up when the no doubt bitter pills light up on his tongue. He swallows hard. I push the water toward him, he pushes it back, spilling half of it onto the table, soaking the paper placemats. He stirs the vegetable soup and very carefully drains a spoonful of green beans and a tiny square of pale orange carrot of all broth. He chews this one spoonful, sets down the utensil, and resumes staring out the window.

And that was lunch.

"Maybe you'll want a hot dog at the ballpark this afternoon?" I nestle two bottles of water into the console between us, and I uncap his. The exhibition game starts in an hour, and the way things are going, I'll need all the extra time to navigate him through the entrance. I'd been looking forward to the game. I'm realizing this was a mistake.

Like when I'd looked forward to taking Jen's kids fishing when they were first and second graders. I didn't drown the first worm—my worm dangled dry and crispy at the end of my hook by the time we finished. What I did do was bait, unhook, restring, and untangle. Over and over again.

The kids had a blast. I had a crash course in keeping children out of a pond.

I won't be watching baseball today. I'll be watching Dad. Expectations are awful things. I should learn not to have any.

"Maybe a hot dog." He reaches for the water bottle, and I try not to react. To not draw attention that I'm paying attention. Like playing with my nieces and nephews, hoping for a certain behavior from a toddler. Mind games. "My son likes baseball."

I remember what Anna said about arguing. And the bits and pieces of what Jen has told me over the years, but I'd not processed it before. Arguing isn't going to help. "Yes, Hayes likes baseball, Dad."

He smiles at me and abandons the water bottle. Not one sip taken.

"I'd like to read a newspaper today."

"Tell me what day it is, and I'll see if I can find a current one." I decide to test him.

"You tell *me* what day it is." He grins. More games. Okay.

"You're wearing blue, so it must be…"

He looks down at his chest and nods. "It's Thursday."

"Good. We'll look for a paper to take with us into the ballpark."

"Good."

"Thirsty, Dad?" I tap one of the bottles.

"I've made a deal with God, you know. Have I told you about our deal?"

"Yeah, Pop. You've told me."

"Tomorrow I wear red. Tomorrow is Friday."

I go silent. He goes silent. I focus on the road and the insanity that is my life. I think about that fishing day with Kerri and Hayes, Jen's two oldest kids named after Aunt Karen and me, Uncle Hayes. She stopped naming her children after family members when those family members started showing their true colors and disappointing the universe with their un-adult-like ways. Little Karen slowly became Kerri. Hayes was stuck with my name, though. I try to be a good uncle. To spend time and do uncle-y things.

Now, thinking back, all my tries seem selfish. I'm not there for them to be there. I'm there to check off an obligatory visit. Like I've been doing with Dad.

So I can get back to my job and my dating life and my…

Maybe that's why I'm not married. The women I date wisely peg me as the selfish obligor that I am and head for the hills. Spreading the word about Hayes Tandy on their way up said hills to all other potential partners.

Maybe it's best I'm alone.

The sound of Dad's noggin against the window glass pulls me back to the car. I tug him up a little straighter so he won't hit his head again. He's slipped into a sound nap—at least I hope it's a nap—and his head wobbles down onto his chest, his glasses sliding down his nose and his lips slightly open. I guess the good thing is that he's not hydrated enough to drool onto his sweater vest.

So I won't have that mess to clean up.

Selfish.

~

As we pull into the ballpark lot, I smell it. I hope it's fumes and not solids, but I can't be sure until I wake him up and pull him from the car.

"Dad, you gotta help me out here."

"What are we doing here? Where's that girl of mine?" I've no idea who he's talking about. Maybe Jen. Maybe Anna. More likely Karen, his favorite, albeit incompetent, daughter. "I smell something."

"You smell you, Dad."

"Where am I?"

"At the ballpark, Pop. Come on, stand up." He's weak and paler than when I'd loaded him into the car at the diner. And as he stands, I see he's had a true accident when he turns his back to me and leans on the door frame. A faint, dark stain is spreading across his rear end.

I moan. I'd asked Anna about this. She assured me toileting wasn't an issue, so I didn't expect this.

Expect. Here I go again.

"Dad, I don't think we're gonna make it to the game today. We need to get you somewhere to clean up." I glance around. We're in the middle of a parking lot that's filling fast. Bright blue portable cesspools line the far edge of the parking lot. "No way."

He starts to get back into the car, but I take his arm and face him toward me, shutting the car door behind him. "No, wait. I need to put something down on the seat first." I lean him back on the hood of the car gently, trying not to think of what I might be smashing in his boxers and against my paint job.

"My son likes baseball. Do you think there's a paper somewhere?"

I ignore his comment and pop the trunk where I have an emergency blanket stowed. That's what I'd learned while dating Pam, the ski instructor. Always be prepared. Even for a Nashville blizzard. I wasn't prepared for that breakup. Or to hear her tell me I needed to work on my people skills. Red flags everywhere and I didn't pay attention to my role in anything.

I dump the contents out next to his black suitcase. I find the mylar emergency blanket and break it out of its package. It's much larger than I expected, and the slight breeze takes the lightweight silver material and flops it around my legs and the bumper.

Baseball fans and their families stare at this oddity.

As they drive by looking for a parking space.

As they exit their vehicles and make their way across the lot.

To scale those steps toward the ballpark and enjoy an afternoon of America's greatest pastime. A game I most certainly won't see. And no hot dogs, either.

They watch as I untangle myself from the blanket, sweat pouring from everywhere and wad the mess under my arm. I salute to one gawking teenager and he quickens his steps.

I open Dad's car door and tuck the rattling material around the seat and down between the edges. Dad's dazed. As if he could fall asleep right there leaning against the car. It's too warm for him to be wearing so many layers. Especially since he's not drinking.

While he's standing, I decide to lighten his clothing a bit. "Here Dad, raise your arms."

He jars his eyes from their haze and meets mine. I remove his glasses from his face and tuck one earpiece into the front of my shirt, letting the red spectacles dangle from my tee. I guide his arms into the air.

I take the rim of the sweater vest, ready to pull it over his head, but he brings his arms down hard, knocking my hands away when the vest is halfway up his torso. "No! I wear blue on Thursdays."

"It's hot. You're a soiled mess. Let me help you."

"I dress myself, young man." He starts to unbutton his trousers. I grab his hands. He wrestles against me, pulling away. He's not a weak man, not in this moment anyway.

I feel an audience growing behind me, real or imaginary, I dare not look. I hear muffled conversations and shoes padding slowly. Then padding quickly. More muffles. I imagine the phone cameras recording, sending this pathetic parking lot interaction viral by midnight.

I beg now. Plead. "Dad. No. Get in the car, and we'll find a place to…"

"No!" He turns so quickly that I can't catch him, my feet tangled in a dangling piece of mylar blanket that I didn't get tucked all the way under the car seat. I trip, falling hard to my knees. The asphalt's heat slaps me in the face before I register the pain in my patella.

My fall has also broken the lenses out of Dad's glasses. The empty red frames glare at me from the blacktop.

When I dare to look up, Dad is several parking spaces away, between a red-neck rusty green pickup and a yellow Prius. "Pop, no!"

Before I can stand, Dad drops his drawers—boxers and all. The edge of his worn-out sweater vest lacks an inch of covering his worn-out manhood. A combo platter of rage and pity well up in me simultaneously.

Then I hear the siren.

~

Some well-meaning and slightly concerned onlooker dialed 911, thinking me an abuser. Or elder abductor.

After clearing up our story with the cops and the EMTs, and after they did their due diligence calling The Pines and corroborating my tale, they got to work on Dad. I warned them he'd become belligerent if they tried to make him drink. They tried anyway.

I'd retrieved Dad's case from the trunk and handed it over to the EMT for a change of clothes. I figure I'll let them handle this part. Maybe he'll cooperate with these strangers better than with me.

I'm a stranger. Maybe a familiar one, but a stranger nonetheless.

I stand at Dad's side as he sits on the tailgate of the ambulance. The engine is running and ice-cold air pours out of the back and envelopes my legs. It has to feel good to Dad too, if he can still process that kind of thing.

"Is there anything I can do for you?" I brush the firefighter's offer aside. My knees will heal. My pride won't.

The EMT offers my father a bottle of water, and he knocks it from the man's hand. I limp a few steps into the parking lot to pick up the bottle. How awful this disease process is.

I watch as Dad cooperates while the EMTs clean him up. I watch as they dress him from the waist down. I watch as they dab the brown stains from the back of his sweater vest, and how they let him keep it on to avoid a meltdown.

I admire their patience and thoughtfulness. Their skill. Their nonjudgmental way of handling such a mess.

I admire these qualities I'm greatly lacking in.

Dad needs much more care than I can give him even on a dumb weekend pass. Or that Jen could even provide. He's full-time care. Dad likely never realized he'd left The Pines' grounds.

I look down at my knees. One bloody. One bruised. I fumble with his glasses and realize that I need to allow the ambulance to transport him back to the Pines. The time for making memories and meaningful connections expired long ago. And I'm the biggest loser on the planet.

I hear one EMT beg my father to drink and a slight threat to start an IV if he doesn't. This won't end well. I have an idea.

The firefighter heads back to his rig. I call after him. "Hey, wait."

"Yessir?"

"Can you make it rain?"

I settle Dad into his bed after Anna dresses him in his blue Thursday night pajama bottoms and white tank top. Our extended weekend pass lasted less than twenty-four hours.

I hand him the newspaper I'd stopped for while the EMTs fiddled with him in the ambulance.

Anna hands him a plastic lidded mug with a straw. I hear the ice sloshing around inside. "That's amazing, what you did for him today."

She wouldn't think it amazing if she knew all the doubts and negativity I was battling.

"The firefighters were awesome," I whisper. They'd positioned their truck behind the ambulance and shot water over the top. Dad brightened up, praising God above for the rain and drank two bottles of water before even leaving the parking lot. I'd stood there, a grown man in his right mind—at least I think I'm in my right mind—and cried as the bright sun painted a rainbow against the hose's shower over the ambulance. Cried as I watched my Dad experience an end to the drought. Cried as I realized he'll likely not remember this tomorrow.

I'll visit him more often. Help out Jen more. Now that I've seen. Now that I know better.

I situate the lens-less glasses on his wrinkled, happy face and try not to cry for the second time today. He takes a long sip from the straw. I pat Dad's face and feel his stubble. Anna promises me he'll be shaved tomorrow. I rub my face. I need a shave too.

I say my goodbyes after I tuck his now-empty black suitcase into the back of the closet and run my hands over his row of button-ups and holey sweater vests. When I look back at the bed, Dad is staring at the upside-down paper through broken glasses.

As I walk down the hallway past other rooms I wonder how bad off the other residents are. How screwed up their families might be. I wonder why no one cares that the hall smells like day-old diapers.

Panic seizes in my chest. I wonder if dementia is in my future.

I wonder what home my extended family will throw me into. If it will smell like diapers or if I'll even have a sense of smell. The ugly picking-the-home job will likely fall to worn-out Jen or maybe to my namesake nephew. I hope to God it doesn't fall to Karen. She'll let me wander the streets naked and soiled, the whole time telling me I'm not nuts.

Anna calls after me, "Have a good weekend, Mr. Tandy. And don't worry about your dad. I'll take good care of him." I nod my thanks. I wonder who *my* Anna will be.

I shove my hands into my shorts' pockets and feel the two unused baseball tickets.

I toss the tickets into the garbage can outside of The Pines' entrance and wonder what color of sweater vest I'll demand to wear on any given Thursday.

Recon

Ava Duncan's had enough. Enough of poor care. Enough of being treated like an invalid and a burden. Enough. But when she embarks on a mission for her own well-being, the suffering of those around her is too much to bear. And then Ava's mission objective changes...

A va Duncan kept her head down, chin to chest, and her eyes closed—a posture she'd observed during her year-long reconnaissance. A recon mission ticked off the calendar one day per week until she could recon no longer and something had to be done. Thirty years in the FBI, Quantico, undercover work, professoring and one shoot-out (she was the backup, not the lead agent that night) and *this* undercover job surpassed in difficulty those thirty years combined.

And no pay for this one. Well, not in the monetary sense, anyway.

She'd parked her wheelchair catty-cornered to the communal dining table. Too eloquent a parking job, and her ability may show, and she couldn't have that. She'd arrived at the right time. By the aromas wafting between stale urine and antiseptic, broccoli and hot dogs. Boiled, of course. Everything was boiled beyond discernible texture in these places, but no amount of boiling could squelch the stench of near-burnt broccoli. Green-smocked and maroon-scrubbed staff members tripped over themselves and the residents to serve the trays, complete with a dollop of lemon pudding, before the main course cooled to room temperature, then, somehow, sucked the cold from the oak table and became near-frigid, despite the air conditioning suffering to keep up with the summer's heat.

Ava was far too familiar with cold food even before she needed extra care. Cold food was given before the stroke. The stroke had taken her left side and, although therapy helped some, her arm was more noodle than functioning appendage. Long nights on stakeouts, eating stale pizza. Overnighters in the conference room at Headquarters with take-out containers littering the table and trashcans full of Styrofoam coffee cups.

She'd take that nasty Chinese and cardboard pizza pie over the care she'd received at home. Her daughter swore she'd watch over Ava. Diane swore to it. But Ava had been left to fend for herself while Diane took the retirement cash to Vegas. Then to Atlantic City. Then to Orlando.

She'd needed the break from caretaking, she'd said.

Needed some time to herself. Ava was a burden.

And the replacement help Diane had hired—with Ava's money, of course—proved to be subpar to even Diane's pathetic attempts at watching over her mother.

Ava inhaled sharply at the intrusion of bitterness. All that training. All that heart-hardening on the job had taught her to channel those emotions into action. Into something doable. But not a day went by when Ava didn't long for the times of cold pizza and ice cream after a victory.

Ava ventured a peek around the room. One hurried gal was straightening the residents' wheelchairs and walkers. Ava's was next. Another employee wrestled—rather roughly—an old guy into a sit-up-straight position.

"Hello, sweetheart. Better wake up." Ava felt her chair reposition and her legs disappeared under the table. The girl gently lifted Ava's face by the chin. Ava kept her eyes half-closed. "You must be the new admit. What's your name, sweetie?"

Ava muttered something under her breath at the condescending sing-song tone of the worker. Sweetheart. Sweetie. Ava wondered how many elderly people really enjoyed being spoken to like toddlers.

Ava didn't mutter a name. Just a grunt. The girl kept going on. "Well, you have a great lunch and we'll get you all squared away soon, okay?" A tray slid in front of her. The gal removed the lid and Ava was smacked in the face with humidity from the rapidly cooling meal.

Ava reached her right arm up and played with her fork—another carefully thought-out move developed over months of watching other residents in six different facilities. How to eat like you need help. How to slouch. How to blend in. How to avoid being talked to by staff.

Drool, even, if that's what it took.

She took a few bites of this and that. Chewed slowly. Nourishment. Keep going until the heat dies down from her disappearance. She'd give Diane until bedtime before the woman realized her mother had skipped. She'd give this facility a week, then she'd order her Uber and find more suitable accommodations further upstate. That was the plan. She'd scouted out the nurse's station. Unmanned a majority of the time. A phone sitting within easy reach of a seated old woman in a wheelchair. She'd watched dozens of times over the last few weeks as visitors and employees left out the side doors and the main door. The same four-digit number unlocked them all.

No one in this place knew Ava didn't belong. Just like that last undercover job. The FBI had won that one. No one in that nightclub had known who Ava was then, either.

And no one in this place knew Ava was sitting on a load of cash.

Literally.

Her seventy-two-year-old, five-seven frame drooped over and guarded a hidden compartment in the seat of the wheelchair. Another skill she'd picked up in the FBI. Slicks. Hiding spots. Cache creations so that no one could out your secrets. She pushed away her tray and repositioned her pelvis. Sitting for too long hurt, but she had no choice.

She lifted her right hand—slowly to avoid attention—and adjusted her head covering—a wrap she'd kept from when her sister died. Bright green background with hot pink hearts. Sis wanted to be buried in the lilac-covered one after that failed round of chemo. Probably best. Lime green would've looked awfully bright poking above the rim of Marie's black casket.

Ava had kept the lime one for herself. A reminder to appreciate the days. Seize the moments.

To abandon what doesn't work for what does.

And she had a feeling this was going to work. A long recon leading to a long con. She'd learned from the best of both worlds. Elite law enforcers and high-rate criminals.

She'd cried after she'd shaven off two years of growth. Then she'd laughed at herself when she put the wrap on her naked scalp this morning. Laughed because she looked ridiculous. Cried again because she felt she was disgracing Marie's battle by looking like a cancer patient. Laughed again when she'd remembered what a spitfire Marie had been, and that likely Marie had approved from her heaven-side stadium bleacher-view of all Ava's reconnaissance and self-preserving plans. The whole escapade would've brought massive joy to her sister. Marie never really got along with Diane, anyway.

The bandana itched, or maybe it was the prickly scalp, and Ava wondered how Marie stood the thing all those months. Maybe Marie's mind was elsewhere, and not on her noggin. Ava's hair could have been donated to Locks of Love if anyone out there really wanted split-ended, mousy gray. Ava doubted that was in style and cleaned up her mess with her right arm as her left arm watched. Careful to remove all traces of the haircut in the "mother-in-law suite" attached to Diane's living room, she'd bagged the locks and stuffed them alongside her siphoned-off cash into the secret compartment of her wheelchair. She'd dispose of the hair later, just before bed.

She'd surveyed the staff here at the great Willowy Way Rehab for quite some time. Several visits a week while Diane was at work or at rest. She'd call the HandiVan service. The driver would help her find a seat on the bus. No need for a wheelchair on these outings—Ava didn't need one. That came later when she'd casually scored a keeper from the Sunrise Center across town. One that had no owner's marking or name. One that could be retrofitted with the compartments she'd need.

Ava gave the drivers the destinations. Sometimes Willowy. Sometimes Sunrise. Sometimes one of the others in the county. She'd kept meticulous notes on a piece of lined paper in her pocketbook. Hand-written. Shorthand. Another tradecraft. Only she could decipher the code. And it didn't hurt that she'd ran intelligence reports on facilities back in the day, a chain that owned a hundred such locations across the country had racked up reports of neglect and abuse. Reports of health code violations. Insurance fraud.

Sad really. It was the fraud that brought the investigation. Not the abuse.

Only Ava knew which rehab centers were well-run. Those she'd need to avoid lest she be discovered before she could get out of the county.

Only Ava knew which centers were grossly understaffed and would likely have a paperwork/personnel failure enough to hide her.

Ava then dealt with the HandiVan Drivers. She'd slip them a tip and a coy little wink as they dropped her back to Diane's and, to Ava's knowledge, not one of those good fellows ever had spoken with Diane. Never tattled on the poor old woman's ramblings and outings over the last year.

The day she'd stolen the wheelchair, she'd not used the same service to get her home. She'd called a different senior transportation company and, sitting slumped in the chair, chin to chest, the driver had graciously loaded up the nearly perfectly abled Ava and her new ride into the van and took her back to Diane's.

Diane never questioned where the chair came from. A fine daughter, that Diane.

Ava resumed the chin-to-chest posture and pushed slightly away from the table into the path of a worker, who dutifully gripped the push handles of the chair and wheeled Ava down the hall to an empty space meant for someone else.

Not meant for able-minded Ava.

The mattress nearest the hallway had been stripped down to the bare black rubber covering. A single dresser opposite the foot of the bed held a small box television. A thin, dangling curtain, stained yellow and brown along the hem, separated one tiny living space from the next. Ava saw the crippled feet of her new roommate pointing at the ceiling peeking from under a thin blue blanket. The roommate's television flashed images of John Wayne and horses. The window above the pour soul's bed should've been scrubbed five years ago. June's bright sunlight couldn't penetrate the grime.

Fifty beds in this facility. Always hiring. Always requiring that staff pull double and triple shifts to cover the cleaning and care and feeding of the aged. This facility and another one across town had made the list for the worst centers in the city. Only the most desperate—or uncaring —of families shipped their charges here. "Restroom?" the girl asked. "Better get it while it's empty. You and Rose share a bathroom with the room across the hall."

Well, Ava had missed that bit on her recon. One restroom for four mobility-hindered elderly people. Fabulous.

This part—Ava cherished her privacy—she'd dreaded from the beginning. Ava nodded yes and allowed the girl to wheel her into the handicapped bathroom. Handrails and pull cords everywhere. Raised toilet seat. Open shower—large enough for three people to stand because that's what it took to bathe another adult body properly without letting the sudsy body slide to the ceramic tile in bone-breaking agony.

Ava allowed the girl to support her under her armpits, drop her drawers, and place her on the commode. "Call me when you're done. I'll get your bed made up. What do you like to watch on TV?" She placed the pull cord in Ava's hand. Ava shook her head yes and grunted. "Well, then. We'll see what Hallmark has on today."

Ava'd rather watch something with a little more elbow grease. A little grittier to remind her of the heydays with the Bureau. And no westerns, thank you very much, but she let that one go. Only four days here. She could do without her crime shows for four days.

Ava hurried up her business. She knew the bathroom issues would come with the territory. The violation of personal privacy is a small price to pay. But it wouldn't be for much longer. After taking care of things herself, Ava let the cord dangle and stood up to stretch. How good it felt to work out the kinks from sitting for so long. She stretched her right arm above her head, then used the right to help the left do the same, continuing the strengthening exercises given to her by the physical therapist.

She wondered how many other unable-bodied souls were pulling on cords throughout the pathetically staffed facility, waiting for their rescue from their porcelain thrones. Ava had heard the bells chiming in the hall on the way to her room. Everyone needed something from someone else.

Everyone but Ava. Ava just needed time.

She dropped her pants again, retook the commode, and pulled the drawcord. A light cased in brittle yellow plastic blinked above the door, letting Ava know the cord had worked. She wasn't sure if her aide knew or not.

Ava calmed her breathing as she waited. She could hear the lady rustling bedclothes. She heard the pop of a tube television coming to life. Channels flipping. Pausing.

"Oh, wow. Ladies. I hope ya'll don't know this one. Another Silver Alert."

The aide swung the door open, and in a rough, too-quick swoop, the girl had Ava covered up and back in the chair. Ava tried to roll her shoulders to counter the burn from the move. She was left facing the television when the other woman's moans pulled the staff worker behind the curtain.

Ava looked at the digital clock blaring its red numerals from the bedside table. Two p.m.

That was fast.

Her own face stared at her from the television. Rather, the face of what she'd been years ago. Shoulder-length dark gray hair, designer glasses, crisp white shirt under a black blazer. Smart looking senior, she was. It was her retirement photo. White letters scrolled across the bottom of the screen over a red banner: *Missing. Presumed to be in danger. Call the tip line.*

Diane couldn't even find a recent photo. Even if Ava hadn't ditched the glasses and the hair, she'd never be recognized by that image. Ava reached up and adjusted her cap again, a slow, steady grin started to spread across her cheeks. Then halted when the aide pulled the curtain open to the wall. "I told you, Rose. You've gotta pull the cord before you have accidents." She wrestled the woman this way and that, as a brown smudge began on the woman's pink gown and white sheet, darkening as it went and fouling up the room.

"A little help in here!" the aide yelled. Ava startled and nearly stood, reaching for her waistline—where there was no gun. And hadn't been for a while. All the recon and planning had her hyper-vigilant. From experience, she knew that'd take a while to calm down after she found herself some new facility.

An employee ducked her head in the room. "I've got my hands full. Do it yourself or wait, Mel."

Mel put her gloved hands on her hips and glared down at Rose. Ava wasn't sure if Rose was cognitive enough to process what was happening in the moment, let alone have the foresight to push a call button or pull a cord before an accident happened. Ava could help. She could rise from the wheelchair and give Mel a hand in cleaning up the old woman and changing the bed.

But Ava was undercover.

The hardest part for her on any mission was to remain undercover when she knew she could do good in the heat of things. That young lady in the nightclub. Agent Duncan could've done something. But the mission outweighed the momentary misery. Four days here was the plan. A plan she'd coded out on paper and then committed to memory.

A deep moan snapped Ava from her thoughts. Mel had managed to roll Rose onto her side so the woman faced the window and her bare back faced Ava—and whoever else cared to walk into the room. Bedsores. From the shoulders to the buttocks, deep and oozing. Combined with the mess the woman had made, Ava nearly vomited her boiled broccoli.

You're undercover, Ava. Don't, just don't.

She used her right hand and feet to maneuver the wheelchair to the doorway and into the hall, trying to keep her head down. Maybe she could ask for help if she loitered in the hallway. Moan and point until someone got Mel out of the way.

The scene in the hall was escalating, rivaling that in her room. A traffic jam of wheelchairs behind her, waiting in line for various shared bathrooms. One gentleman's catheter bag had overflowed, a yellow puddle spread over the tile under him.

Four days. Only four days.

The woman who'd refused to help Mel approached the old guy and jerked him by the arm. Ava heard a snap, and the old man's foggy blue eyes welled with tears.

No way.

Diane may be a neglectful thief, but nothing could compare to this. Ava couldn't take it.

She did what she'd told herself for a year that she'd never do.

She blew her cover.

She stood, stretched, and pushed her own empty wheelchair to the unmanned nurse's station and dialed 911. She turned herself in.

Gave the dispatcher the location of the nursing home.

Gave the dispatcher a rundown—so at least there was a voice recording—of what she'd witnessed in a few hours at Willowy.

Then she threatened to spill every secret that she'd locked away from her years in the FBI if they didn't send someone.

Posthaste.

Ava returned the receiver to its cradle and turned to face the open dining and visiting area. A half dozen residents, chins to chests, slept out in the open. Sitting straight up in their chairs. Better that than face the unkind, overworked hands of the help.

How did she miss the gravity of this during her recon? Shame welled in her chest, pressing in on her ribs. She'd broken a cardinal rule of investigation. She'd only seen what she wanted to. What benefited her. She'd justified the state of this place to fit her needs of escaping Diane. Never a thought to the folks who were already here. Day after day. Suffering. Rotting.

Ava rolled her chair to the entry, punched in the four-digit numeric code, and the door buzzed open. Three elderly had gathered at the door. One with a walker. Two in chairs. Ava held it open for them and the four shells of once-thriving souls wheeled/stepped into the breezeway. One old guy grinned up at her from his seat, his lips cracking. Likely the first smile and the first breath of fresh air the fellow'd had in months.

And no one noticed they'd been freed. If only temporarily.

An ambulance fifty feet down in the parking lot unloaded a woman strapped onto a stretcher. Thin, frail, about five-seven. Gray locks of hair in all directions covering the pillow. This woman was likely Rose's intended roommate. Ava took a seat in her chair and watched and prayed for this woman and the plight that awaited her.

Sirens in the distance indicated Ava's recon was up. That's okay. Someone may listen to her now. The drastic measures she'd taken to get away from Diane would hold weight. The state of the facility. The voice recording to the dispatcher. Willowy was part of a chain with a few dozen nursing homes across the country. A larger investigation would be triggered. Ava would see to that.

Her one last mission.

The sirens were louder now, and despite the afternoon glow, The EMTs were catching a clue. Too many old people outside cluttering up the entryway. They couldn't get the stretcher through without ushering them to the side.

A local police car and a black sedan boxed in around the ambulance.

Ava waved at the officers.

Then she waved at the old guy exiting the sedan. Then she cried. It was Rodney.

Her last desk jockey partner.

Ava rolled over to him.

"You can't behave, can you?"

"You won't behave when you retire, either."

"Probably not."

The pair had researched and settled several fraud cases before Ava's stroke. Rodney was close to retirement, as well. Ready for the lake and fishing and grandchildren visits.

He scanned the building and the pale white faces of the charge nurses. Who up until that very moment had no clue what was happening. And likely, up until that very moment, didn't care.

"Diane's worried." Rodney pulled a wooden bench with flaking white paint near Ava's wheelchair and sat down. "Thought you could use a familiar face when we found you. Called me personally. Then the 911—"

Ava laughed. "Diane's not worried. Diane's in Reno."

Rodney hung his head. "Nothing gets by you."

"Miss Ava, sweetie. You'll have to come to the station and give a report." The young police officer bent to her level as if talking to a child who'd stolen a cookie.

"It's Agent Duncan, young man. Mind your manners." She winked at Rodney and rose from her wheelchair, startling the officer. "Keep ahold of that chair. It's got my life savings tucked in the seat."

Rodney's eyes widened as he stood to obey his partner's command. "Yes, ma'am."

The officer helped Ava into the front seat of the squad car. His partner remained behind to herd the old folks back inside—now many more enjoying the warm sunlight than the few Ava had set loose. Ava grinned. This time the grin made it from ear to ear. Her stomach growled. The broccoli and hotdog had burned off.

"Shall we get some pizza before we go back to the station?" She gave the young man the coyest smile she could muster and got a grin in response. With a tiny nod.

Then she winked at him. Patted his kneecap.

That drew a chuckle, a little more gas, a flip of the siren switch.

And the offer of ice cream after.

Penny's Place

When Penny passes away, it falls to Kylie to pick up the slack at the diner—and to take care of Roy, the old geezer who lingers too long and never seems to take a bath.

"It'll be hard on him today." Tyler nodded toward the window at the twelve-passenger van as he filled the acrylic countertop display with fresh-baked rolls. The van operated by the senior center carried citizens with no other means of transportation to and from the grocery store, bank and Penny's Place diner. "I'm glad I'm back here. I wouldn't put up with him the way Penny does—did."

Kylie wished she could trade places with Tyler in the kitchen. Away from all the customers, not just Roy. All morning, condolences had been handed out for the woman Kylie had barely known. Kylie just wanted to work her double shift and go home.

Penny died last week, and the diner had shut down for the funeral. Kylie had only waited tables there for about a month, a job she hated in a town she despised, but after running out of money at college—for tuition and food—she didn't have much of a choice. The rock-bottom rent for her studio apartment was the only bonus Gainesville held for Kylie until she could earn enough cash to return to her graphic design studies at DeLane.

Waitressing, face to face with people all day—that was the last thing that matched Kylie's personality.

Kylie had met Roy on her first day. Evidently, he was a regular. She didn't know his name for the first week or so. She was terrible with names and had struggled to keep up with her tables in that first week. Roy always sat at the counter, and Penny always took care of him.

Kylie wiped down a table and put the dollar tip in her back pocket. One dollar closer to saying goodbye to the cornflower blue walls with yellow polka dots the size of dinner plates and endless requests for refills.

That's what she kept telling herself, at least. One dollar at a time.

The bell over the front door banged against the frame, and Roy took his place at the counter seat. The diner ran a waitress short today until Penny's husband could hire more staff, so Kylie had the ten tables and the five seats at the counter.

Penny had had the patience of a saint. She'd always greeted Roy in the same manner. Always put up with him paying in pennies. A joke between the two of them maybe. Penny's Place only takes pennies.

He'd taken a lot of her time, sometimes staying for over an hour for a cup of coffee, and he never left a tip. Well, never a good one. A single penny. No more, no less.

"Why don't you do something about him?" Kylie had Tyler ask Penny one day after Roy boarded the red transit bus. "He smells and no one wants to sit next to him. He's a waste of space."

Penny had rolled up the dishtowel and snapped it at Tyler's leg. "No one is a waste of space. We may be the only social interaction that poor man gets." Tyler had dropped it and no one else had questioned it again.

"What'll it be Roy?" Kylie slung the very same dishtowel, the one with the purple stains from the season's special raspberry pie, over her shoulder and poured the black coffee she knew he'd ask for.

Roy, a good three days past due for a bath, looked confused. He eyed the steaming coffee cup and then eyed Kylie. She sighed impatiently. At least there wouldn't be five people to wait on at the counter. Roy's stench would drive them to a table or out the door.

"Where's Penny?"

"Roy, Penny passed away." The words came out flat. "Remember? Remember last week when you couldn't come to the diner for a few days because we closed down? That was because Penny died."

"Oh." He stared at the coffee and twirled the cup on the saucer.

"Anything else?" Kylie asked as a four-top came through the door. "Roy, is there anything else I can get you?" She already knew the answer.

He shook his head and sipped at the coffee.

Kylie left him at the counter, cleared her nostrils and her impatience with a couple of deep breaths and went to seat the couples.

"Miss, Miss?" She hadn't even taken the drink orders before Roy was calling her back.

"One minute, Roy." She smiled at the table in front of her, took their requests and went to the counter.

"Penny always stayed up here and we talked and stuff."

"Roy, I'm the only one here. Do you see the other table? They need drinks and food, too."

"But Penny never left the counter."

"I'm not Penny, Roy. I'm Kylie." He hung his head like he'd been caught doing something wrong. Kylie cringed and softened. "Look, I'll check on you in a little bit." He barely nodded and she went about serving the other table, along with two more that walked in while she was coddling Roy.

When she got back to the counter, Roy had left. His cup was half-full, still steaming. Forty-nine pennies lay on the right side of the cup. One shiny new penny on the left. Her tip. She went to the door and hung her head out, but Roy was gone.

"Hey, Tyler! Did the transit van pick up Roy?"

"What, he's gone already? What's your secret?"

Kylie frowned. "Yeah, he left, but I didn't see him get picked up." She supposed Roy knew what he was doing. She went about her double shift covering double the real estate in the diner, and Roy was soon forgotten.

Kylie walked the two blocks home to her small studio apartment above the bank, her jean pockets weighed down with dollar bills and quarters. She'd lost track after twenty bucks, but today, with the double, she'd at least be able to afford the electric bill.

She fumbled with the lock on the old door, flipped the lights, threw her keys down and emptied her pockets on the counter. A quick count of her tips and she was satisfied that in a few more days, the month's bills would be covered and the rest of the income could go into her college fund—the fund her parents had stopped funding because she was "irresponsible" and needed to "learn a lesson." If she wanted to finish, she'd have to go it on her own.

She kicked something on the floor and sent it skidding across the kitchen. She couldn't get used to the mail slot and walked right on top of the letters and bills every time she came home.

She gathered the mess, threw away the sales fliers and coupons for fast food. The diner provided one meal per shift. It was peanut butter and jelly the rest of the time.

A hand-addressed letter caught her attention. It was a letter from

Penny's lawyer. Penny had left everyone at the diner a small bonus of a hundred dollars and a personal note. Kylie was shocked. She turned the check over and over. She didn't have a chance to get to know Penny at all outside of training. The other employees had worked with her for years. She opened the letter.

Dear Kylie,

I'm sorry we didn't get a chance to know each other. I'm sure you'll do great at the diner. Gainesville is lucky to have someone like you.

Penny.

P.S. Take care of Roy for me, will you?

Kylie stared at the note and read it several times. Lucky to have someone like her? Penny hadn't even known her. If she'd had any idea how Kylie truly felt about the small town and the dumb diner, she'd have never included Kylie in the bonus. Or taken the time to write the note.

And take care of Roy? It made her dread her double shift tomorrow even more. And all the penny-counting she'd have to waste her time with.

She scooped up the loose change from the countertop and dumped it into a large glass bowl in the bottom of her closet. A few boxes from college packed neatly away for her return trip lined the bottom, and then she had an idea.

A few semesters ago, Kylie's sorority had held a coin drive for a community project at DeLane. No one had wanted to fool with counting money, so the girls had sprung for a battery-operated coin counter. Dump the coins in the top and the digital readout did the rest. She dug through the boxes until she found the machine and flipped it on.

Nothing.

Well, a quick stop to the corner market in the morning for a fresh set of batteries was a small price to pay for all the time she'd save counting Roy's dumb change. She retrieved a few loose dollars to pay for the batteries in the morning, changed into her pajamas and crashed for the night.

~

Right on the money, the bell above the door rang as the transit van pulled away. Roy took his place at the counter.

"Hey, Roy. Coffee?" Kylie tried to keep the words short and to the point. If she opened the door for conversation, he'd walk all the way in and overstay his welcome.

He smiled and nodded.

"Penny's gone, isn't she?"

Kylie offered a half sympathetic grin as she poured his coffee. "Yes, she's gone."

"And you're Kylie?" He took a sip.

"Yep. All day every day."

He almost choked as he chuckled and gave her a grin.

"Need anything else?"

He shook his head. "Not too busy today? You stay at the counter? Talk a while?"

Kylie shifted and grabbed a washcloth. "I've got to get ready for the breakfast rush, Roy."

"Oh." He started fishing pennies, one by one, from his pocket.

"Hey, that reminds me. Since I'm working out here alone, I thought this might help." She pulled the coin sorter from behind the counter and carefully showed Roy how to work it. "That way, you can help save me some time. You put your pennies for your coffee in here. This tells you how many you've paid."

Roy lit up and grinned a yellow, ragged smile from ear to ear. He spent the next fifteen minutes feeding the machine pennies. Kylie went about tidying things and waiting on a couple of stragglers.

"Got it figured out?"

"Forty-nine. On the dot." He put one extra penny beside the machine. Kylie's tip. "This was a nice thing you did for me."

"I'm not so nice, Roy. Just trying to get work done."

"It's nice to know someone was thinkin' about me when I wasn't nowhere near them."

Kylie shifted uncomfortably and tried not to make eye contact.

"You're not too busy right now. Want to have some coffee with me?"

"Honestly, no. I don't want to." Since the coin sorter went well, she thought maybe she could solve another problem. "Quite honestly, Roy," she lowered her voice, "you need a bath."

He looked surprised, then reared back his head and belly-laughed. She could smell his foul coffee-laden breath from behind the counter.

"That's probably right. Probably right. But, usually, baths are for church-goin' and funerals." He laughed again and fished another penny from his pocket and left it next to the machine with the first one. "We'll see, Kylie. We'll see." The transit van pulled to the curb and honked, and Roy left, leaving his aroma to linger over the counter.

Tyler poked his head around the corner. "Betcha wish you stayed at DeLane."

Kylie would've snapped the towel at him, but she didn't know how.

The next day, Roy showed up in clean clothes. Clothes Kylie had never seen him wear. The overalls were gone. He wore a white oxford button-up and black trousers that jingled with pennies when he walked in the door. Kylie, Tyler and a couple of regular customers did a double-take.

Roy had even trimmed up his beard.

She went to the counter and poured him his coffee. She set the coin sorter next to him. He smiled with still-yellow teeth, but she couldn't smell his breath. All she could pick up was the steaming black coffee.

"Wow, Roy. You clean up nice!"

"It was a chore. It was a chore." He sipped the coffee and turned the cup in the saucer. "I suppose you're busy today."

"I suppose. But you holler if you need anything, okay Roy?"

He nodded and worked on the coffee.

Kylie went about waiting and bussing tables. She enjoyed the extra money the doubles were putting in her account, but the diner really needed another pair of hands, even if it meant sharing the tips.

When she had a moment to look up, Roy was gone. One penny on the counter. Forty-nine in the machine.

Roy didn't come back the next day. Or the day after that. Tyler hadn't seen him. After her shift on his fourth absence, Kylie flagged down the transit van and quizzed the driver, but it was his first day back after an illness, so he didn't know anything.

"Why didn't the transit company check on him?" Penny's note rang through Kylie's brain. As much as she didn't want to deal with Roy, she could feel his absence in the pit of her stomach. "Can you take me to his home, uh…" She struggled to read his embroidered name tag.

"Joe. Name's Joe. Get on." Joe nodded sheepishly to the fare box. Kylie rolled her eyes and deposited four quarters from her tips.

It took twenty minutes to get to Roy's tiny home on a dilapidated lot. Weeds grew in the landscaping and paint chipped off the siding. Kylie asked Joe to wait, since there was no one else on the van, and he was happy to do so.

She knocked on the door. Then she tried the door handle. The door swung open with a creak and Roy's familiar odor smacked her in the face.

She coughed a little before announcing herself. But there was no answer. She worked her way through the barren entry and checked some of the rooms, but Roy was not there.

She went out the back door and saw him sitting in an old metal rocker facing the back of the property. A tall oak tree dwarfed the house and the yard.

"Hey, Roy!"

He didn't turn around.

She approached him, and then she understood. He sat there, holding a brown leather book in ash gray hands. He'd shaved again and had on a crisp blue oxford with black trousers.

Church and funerals. Roy had cleaned up to go home.

Kylie had never seen a dead person before, at least not one out of a casket. She called for Joe, who stumbled through the yard. Joe fumbled with his phone and called 911.

Her head spun. She should've checked on him the first day he didn't show. She sat down with her back to the oak tree, staring at Roy just sitting in that chair, his head bowed down to his chest.

Emergency crews came and went. Someone handed her the book that had been in his lap. Joe's arms were around her. Kylie felt guilty, as her first thought was that Joe didn't smell much better than Roy. But she allowed herself to weep with the old driver and then he took her home.

Kylie rode in Roy's seat back to her studio, clutching the brown book.

It wasn't until she was in her apartment and after she'd showered that she realized she shouldn't have taken it. The book was an album filled with photos of people she didn't know.

Or did she?

There was Joe, the kind transit driver. Old Mildred was pictured with a much younger Roy in front of Gainesville Bank, the same one Kylie lived above now. Mildred always complained that the diner pies weren't like the ones that her mother used to make, but ate two slices anyway.

She could make out a few more faces if she imagined them more wrinkled and weathered. Some rode the transit. A few she had to help onto the transit with their doggie bags. She supposed if she'd taken the time to really look at the faces of the riders, she could match more photos with more people. She had to remove the photos and look at the names.

She sobbed again.

She didn't know their names.

As she closed the photo album, two envelopes fell to the floor. One had Penny's name. The other had Kylie's name, but it was misspelled.

Both had faint brown stains from a coffee mug.

Kylie set Penny's aside. She'd give that to Ed tomorrow at the diner. She opened hers and cried again as she read his shaky cursive.

Kilee,

You are nice and don't let anyone tell you otherwise. Penny would be proud of you for helping out an old geezer like me.

Roy

. . .

She turned the envelope upside down and a single penny fell into her lap.

Six months after Roy's funeral, Kylie stood prepped and ready outside Penny's Place for the grand reopening. Even Tyler had spiffed up and wore a chef's hat for the occasion. Joe and Mildred—and way too many people for the number of tables—lined the street all the way to the bank.

Ed came, dressed in a suit. "I'm sure glad you left the name the same." Ed admired the lettering on the window. Kylie had used her graphic design skills to redo the fonts and artwork, but it was still Penny's Place. The menus and business cards had gotten a much-needed update, too.

"I wouldn't think of changing the name. It will always be Penny's Place." She put an arm around his shoulders and led him inside.

Ed hadn't wanted to mess with the diner, he was too old. Kylie, after Roy's death and much soul searching, had decided to take on the role of manager with the option to buy Ed out as soon as she had enough money.

One dollar at a time.

He looked around in stunned silence. The tables were newer, as well as the countertop and display cases. The walls had a fresh coat of paint.

"I tried to match it as close as I could." Cornflower blue walls with yellow polka dots, freshly painted. The only addition to the walls was the photo gallery.

Inside each dot of sunshine was an eight-by-ten photograph, blown up from Roy's album. Under each photo, Kylie had hung a small bronze plate with the names and dates for each image. Several people had died since Kylie had taken over the diner. Some of them were still regulars.

And Kylie knew them all by name.

Shortages

Ada Kenworthy is content with her home and her hoard, sipping tea alone and keeping to herself. When her aging neighbor asks for help, Ada's spryness surprises her, and she finds an unexpected friend and a secure future in the process.

A da Kenworthy straightened her thin housecoat around her shoulders. Her wrinkled hands smoothed the pale blue seersucker fabric. She tidied up one of the buttons, the cloth had gathered awkwardly, causing the pink of her nightgown underneath to show through. Modest lady always, even alone in the house, alone for ages, she'd never permit the nightgown to show itself in any room other than the bedroom.

She allowed her fingers to inspect the pockets, pockets she'd carefully sewn onto the garment using the old Singer upstairs in a room she'd not seen in years. A tiny hole was starting in the right one. She'd have to dig out her mending kit from under the bathroom vanity and fix it. Someday.

In the left one, she'd tucked a souvenir from her neighbor. If she stood very still, she could hear the ticking from the pocket watch. Eighty years old she may be, but her hearing was keen.

She exhaled deeply as the kettle on the stove whistled, blowing steam into the already humid kitchen. She drew the roller shade closed against the black night outside the window above her table for two. She could feel the tension leave her back and neck as she steeped her teabag and sank into the chair. She'd been chasing this moment the entire day. The entire week, actually. The moment she could breathe, albeit in the dusty corner of her breakfast nook. The moment she could close her eyes and not fear what she'd see when she opened them. That moment when the only sounds were those familiar to her. The ticking of the grandfather clock in the front room. The hum of the refrigerator. The sound of the creaking boards under her feet.

Her kitchen, her entire house, was stuffy, but she'd taken to chilling no matter the heat over the last few years. The central air unit remained idle all summer, as it had the summer before. It would likely never be turned on again so long as she lived here. She didn't mind the stuffiness. It added a layer of protection, like the safety an infant feels when swaddled in flannel. In a few weeks, the leaves would begin dripping coppers and mustards, and the cooler air would seep beneath the cracks in the door and around the windows.

She shuddered and sipped as the chamomile warmed the deep

ache in her bones and belly. As she sipped, the frustrations of the last few days still toyed with her. The folder from the funeral home and packet from the lawyer sat on the table in front of her. They'd been there for nearly a year, and they were likely the only things in the home that had sat for that long that didn't have a layer of living on top of them.

She traced the lacey tablecloth with one hand as the other fiddled with the edge of the folder. She didn't open it. The contents enraged her. The longer she dwelt on it, the more her left foot jumped up and down inside her ragged house slipper. But she was glad for her old slippers. They sure felt better than the boots she'd been forcing her arthritic toes into for the better part of a week.

Another sip of tea. Another deep breath. Her foot stopped bobbing. Her hands relaxed around the smooth porcelain of the teacup. The gentle clank of the cup against the saucer absorbed into the table and walls and brought as much comfort as the tea itself.

Her sounds.

Her sights.

Her smells.

Such a contrast to what she'd faced all week.

The entire ordeal started with a foreign thumping. It had been so long since someone knocked on her door that she'd taken a good thirty seconds to process the sound. Five homes, hers smack in the middle, guarded a crumpling cul-de-sac in a nearly forgotten neighborhood. Mail trucks came daily, but the carrier never knocked and rarely left anything other than bills and bad news. School buses stopped scooping up and dropping off children two decades ago. For three streets in each direction, only the elderly remained. Their extended families dead or forgotten. Families estranged or enmeshed in their own lives rarely, if ever, visited the poor folks of Pebble Drive.

Occasionally an ambulance siren pierced the neighborhood's solitude, but usually that upheaval arrived in silence. No need to hurry for the dead. No need to wake the near-dead either.

And as Pebble Drive has gone, so will go the rest of Stone County. Soon, any remaining children—all high schoolers now—will be bussed two counties over for their education. The Boomers left long ago. The

Millennials want nothing to do with this neck of the county. Their fancy signals and internets and smarty gadgets just don't connect in these parts so far away from the nearest unsightly metal tower.

Ada stood, her knees aching, and shuffled to the overflowing sink with her teacup and saucer. She'd have to buckle down and wash the mess up soon. A dozen fruit flies swirled as she rattled the cup into the sink. She was also short on clean teacups. Maybe Mr. Eplin had some in his cabinet. Maybe she could take those and skip washing the dishes. Leave the flies to the toast crumbs and chamomile and little bits of mud a few days longer.

Poor Mr. Eplin. His fist had been at the other end of the knocking Tuesday, and Mr. Eplin had started this massively stressful week this time last year with a similar pounding on the door.

He was her next-door neighbor. They'd catch sight of each other maybe once a week as they reached out to gather in mail. Sometimes several days' worth of mail at a time, as no resident in the cul-de-sac cared enough to open their rusty boxes every day. What good could come from that?

He'd stood on her porch steps, panicked and gasping, and tried to explain himself. A choppy story flowed from the old man's lips, his disheveled beard trembled with his jaw. His overall strap fell off one shoulder, his slight frame underneath mimicked Ada's—bony and frail, swallowed in clothing too big years ago. His deep-set eyes hadn't rested well in some time. He'd apparently splashed on some Avon aftershave before he walked the short distance between the porches. The poignant aroma took Ada back to her dating days. Old Avon. The kind circling her beaus who'd pick her up for a drive-in movie.

Something deep inside Ada had wanted to invite the old man into her home. To fix him some tea with honey or coffee, black and strong. To pull up a chair in the tiny kitchen and allow him some comfort as he told her of his woes. But she hadn't. Couldn't.

She'd stood, frozen, one shoulder against the doorframe. The other against the edge of the barely opened door.

He hadn't seemed to mind. He remained on the porch. A pest of a horsefly attempted to land on his beard multiple times. He'd not bothered to swat it away. Too distraught over Mr. Frederick. The neighbor on the other side of Mr. Eplin. The ambulance had come. He'd watched from his bathroom window as the EMTs entered the house with a stretcher. They exited with a skinny lump under black plastic. And the poor young men had fallen to their knees, gagging. After the ambulance had pulled away, Mr. Eplin had walked to the front of Mr. Fredrick's home. The mail had gathered in a huge heap. The smell of death lingered down the steps.

The mailman had likely called this in.

And Mr. Eplin didn't want to go the same way. He didn't want to lay for days or weeks before someone noticed he'd not reached outside for his handful of fast food coupons and political mailers. He didn't want his home and his belongings stunk up with decay. Touched by who-knows-whose-hands and thrown into the thrift store giveaway bin.

He'd collapsed in tears. More likely over the collection than over what would happen to him.

He wanted Ada's help. And her word that if something should happen to him, she'd handle his affairs with some air of dignity.

He'd made Ada promise that if she'd not noticed movement around his home, if his mail piled up—which he vowed that day, a year ago, to always get his mail—that she'd do the right thing.

The right thing. Ada sighed again, the stress threatening to creep back up her spine. She shook it off. That was the year-ago-knock.

The this-week-knock had been quite different. When he'd pounded on her door for the second time, she'd had no choice but to let him in, as he fell forward, clutching his chest. His eyebrows rode high above startled orbs, he leaned against the wall, knocking off a shadowbox of decaying butterflies from behind him. She steadied him with one hand and with the other she caught the butterfly box before it busted on the floor. Her spryness startled her, and she'd had to force her attention back to the man in front of her.

Still in slippered feet, she helped him down her porch, his bony arm draped over her shoulders, his hand clutching on. She guided him into his home. He could barely put one foot in front of the other. Through his front room. Through his kitchen...

Another deep breath as Tuesday poured into her mind. Ada had kept her word to the old neighbor and had done the right thing. No ambulance needed. No sirens to disturb the few remaining peaceful residents of Pebble Drive.

She picked up the folder, turned off the kitchen light, and made her way to the recliner in her front room. The glow from the single street-light at the end of the cul-de-sac lit her path just enough for her to fumble with the side-table lamp without knocking anything to the floor. She settled into the worn burgundy recliner, its lumps and dips hugging her frame like an old friend, and raised the legs. She pulled the quilt—also sewn on the old Singer upstairs—over her lap and up around her shoulders. She sat the folder on the arm rest.

The recliner and Ada faced a fireplace that hadn't been lit in three decades. Where logs and kindling should be, washbowls and pitchers, the kind you'd see in antique stores now, nestled inside. Ada had arranged clusters of artificial flowers daffodils, roses, and daisies, inside each pitcher. The blooms were all the same shade of gray-brown from layers of dust. But when Ada looked at them each night as she tucked herself into her recliner—she'd stopped traveling the stairs to the bedroom and the Singer long ago—she could still see the bright yellows, reds, and whites from the day she'd decorated the hollow.

She had dusted the grandfather clock. Mr. Eplin would've liked that she did. He would've liked that she tucked his final gift to her behind the panel that housed the swinging pendulum.

She glanced to the door. The butterfly box still sat on the floor where she'd let it slide down. The monarchs and painted ladies in the box were as faded as the flowers. She knew this. But she could still see the shimmering scales, as fresh as the springtime sun the day she'd found the piece at a yard sale. Ada let her head rest against the back of the chair and allowed her slippers to fall from her feet. She'd not cried over the old man. Likely wouldn't. They hadn't been friends. They hadn't been friendly. Just there. Next to each other for years. Each cocooned in their own environments.

Ada's home was cluttered with all manner of randomness collected with fervor until the money and the energy ran out and she was left with a dusty horde of odds and ends that only she could appreciate. Each bobble and knickknack and random furniture piece held a part of her. She'd had no children. No family. The items in her home were surrogates, though at the time she purchased and lugged them home, she'd not thought of them in that way. Now, though. If something went missing, well, she'd certainly shed some tears.

She'd have cried if the shadowbox had busted.

And Mr. Eplin's home, well... *he* was obsessed. That first trip through his house a year ago. The second trip through his home Tuesday. The third Wednesday...

She shook her head at the thought of it, pushed her glasses into their proper spot on her nose, and opened the folder on her lap. The lawyer's card was tucked in one side along with Mr. Eplin's will. What a waste of time that had all been. The lawyer had been kind enough to meet the old neighbors in Mr. Eplin's home, take his money for drafting the will, and to drive them to Stone County Funeral Parlor to leave them to deal with the meanest man in the county by themselves.

Ada shook her head again and tossed the lawyer's card to the floor onto a pile of junk mail that she'd get around to throwing out. Someday. Ada had never dealt with the business of death. Never gave it much thought. Never had to bury a husband or a child. She'd only attended her parents' funerals. And one brother who'd died young. But she'd never been the one to plan. And she'd never been back to Stone County Cemetery to pay her respects.

"Shortages, Ms. Kenworthy. Shortages. That's all I can say."

"But his wishes, sir. He wants his collection to be buried with him."

Mr. Eplin had remained silent. Gray-blue eyes hid behind a shroud of tears that threatened to trace the wrinkles on his cheeks the further the conversation went.

"That's just not possible, I'm afraid." Apparently, the only cemetery in the county was full up, minus five spots. No more land to acquire for the ever-growing aged death toll. The funeral home recommended cremation. It was the way Mr. Frederick had gone, and that should be good enough for Mr. Eplin as well, the curmudgeonly funeral director had explained. "I can sell you a spot, a single spot just for you. I can sell you all five spots. And you can fill them with whatever, but for what you're explaining, it's just not possible."

"I want my things with me. Not spread out all over the hillside."

Ada knew she should reach over and pat the old man's shoulder or knee, give him a little comfort. But they weren't friends and she didn't want him to get the wrong idea. Modest lady that she was.

"What about digging deeper? Or longer? Or…"

"Ms. Kenworthy, that's just not feasible. We could run into someone else's headstone if we dig longer. We could hit a water aquifer and flood the whole place if we dig deeper. No, I'm sorry. All the counties around here are dealing with such shortages."

Ada looked at Mr. Eplin, refrained from patting him, but said, "Let's go. We'll call for a ride back to Pebble Drive and figure this out later." He'd agreed. They'd called for the Handi-Van service that hauled the non-driving aged ones to banks and doctors and markets. Their county, poor as it was, could afford just the one van.

Shortages.

She had a favorite driver. Turns out Mr. Eplin, did too. The same kid. Well, a kid to them, more like a middle-aged guy who, given his record and the shortage of employment in these parts, was forced to haul old bones to and fro.

The van was empty, and for that Ada was glad. The couple sat in seats across the aisle from each other. Ada didn't want Harley to get the wrong idea if she'd chosen to sit right next to Mr. Eplin, even if she'd wanted to. Harley started with polite small talk, but, through the oversized rearview mirror, he spotted Mr. Eplin's distress and asked what the trouble was. Ada would've kept her business to herself, but Mr. Eplin's long, bad day came spilling out in between sobs. Harley listened as he wound the van through quiet streets and humble neighborhoods back to Pebble Drive.

He put the van in park and shifted in his seat. "I wouldn't give that rotten lawyer nor the funeral home any of your hard-earned money, Gil."

"Well, I have to be put somewhere." Mr. Eplin, Gilbert—Ada never called him or even thought of him by his first name, they weren't friends, anyway—rubbed a liver-spotted hand over his overalls bib. "I don't have much time left. I can feel it ticking away."

"We'll have to come up with another plan. Do some more research." Harley helped them maneuver the steps.

"But how?" Mr. Eplin's voice was distraught as Ada's thoughts. If he did die, now there was legal paperwork that meant Ada had to deal with it. By herself. She wanted Harley's answer as badly as Mr. Eplin did.

"Care to show me what we're dealing with?" Harley nodded toward Mr. Eplin's home. The old man nearly skipped up the steps, eager to solve his end-of-life trauma before the end caught up with him.

"I'll let you two be. You know where I'm at if you need me." Ada had no interest in walking through Mr. Eplin's home again. The sounds and smells were too much to bear. Ticking and tocking bouncing in a cacophony of unkempt rhythms through the whole place. Front room. Hall. Bathroom. Kitchen. Mr. Eplin had no shortages of clocks. Large ones, small ones, filling every nook and cranny. And, much to Ada's shame, none of them had one speck of dust. Each one meticulously cared for as if they were surrogates for infants or long-lost loves.

Avon aftershave in the bathroom floating down the hall. Air fresheners and carpet powders in the front room. The kitchen smelled of cinnamon and cloves and all of it all together was cause enough for a migraine.

She'd thought of her own dusty, messy hoard. Maybe she should clean up. Even with plain soap and water, cut down on the sharp aromas.

Maybe she'd be able to invite someone in to share tea or coffee at her tiny table for two.

Someday.

"Good day, Miss Ada. Groceries on Friday? Same as usual?" Harley asked as he aimed Mr. Eplin toward the porch steps.

"Yes, Harley. That'd be fine."

And Ada hadn't needed to call Harley for anything but groceries since that day in the front yard. Not until Tuesday. That was the plan. The right thing to do.

She flipped through the documents again. Normally she'd keep things like this until they were buried under other things like this. No matter the dates or when the government says you should or can throw things out. Next to the Singer was a pile of tax returns from forty years ago. The folder should join that pile. But it won't. She let it drop to the side on top of the junk mail. What need did she have of the will now? What need did she have of the numbers for Stone County Funeral Home?

She decided to let it go. She plopped the folder onto the mail pile, dust swirling into the table light's rays. The grandfather clock chimed midnight. Twelve soft bells. She thought of the package nestled behind. "There's money in my clocks, Ada." He'd told her that several times over the course of making his final arrangements. She and Harley had thought that to mean the clocks themselves were worth something and should be sold. But it didn't make sense that he wanted to be buried with them—all of them—if they were worth so much.

All those clocks would've taken up cemetery slots.

And there was a shortage.

And you can't dig deep.

Ada and Harley had chalked this up to old age. The man was running short on time and didn't make much sense.

Harley showed up, as promised, Tuesday evening. Ada had gotten Mr. Eplin all the way to the back door before his old ticker gave its last under the layer of overalls and Avon, and the only thing left was the ticking of his precious clocks. Harley didn't leave Pebble Drive until the sun came up Wednesday morning. All night. Digging under and around the roots of an ancient oak tree that bordered Mr. Frederick and Mr. Eplin's yards. Deep he dug, and wide. Ada helping where she could. Bringing him water from Mr. Eplin's faucet and occasionally retreating to her own back porch and into her kitchen to smell the familiar dust and warmth.

Ada brought out armful after armful of clocks and piled them next to the pit as Harley kept digging. Then she dropped one. And that's the only time she'd nearly cried, from exhaustion and from the disrespect it showed to her old neighbor. But when the back fell off the timepiece, President Grant greeted her in the light of the stars and the streetlamp. Fifty bucks. "Harley."

He stopped digging and picked up another clock, pulling the back off. President Jackson.

President Lincoln.

Mr. Franklin himself.

All stately and proper lying in an ever-growing pile in Gilbert Eplin's backyard.

Harley and Ada worked all night. Digging, opening, lugging.

Laying, placing, covering.

For eighty years old, she was quite the spry woman. Harley had said so many times, and she felt he feared he'd be digging her grave the very same night if she didn't slow down.

They'd split the money, as was only fair. And Ada promised Harley he'd have what was left of hers when she died. And she told him where she'd keep it tucked.

"I've just the one clock, though. None of this nonsense. And a single, simple hole. Not so deep and not so long," Ada'd instructed, and Harley'd agreed. He left his shovels on Ada's back porch. Just in case some Friday she didn't come to the door when he delivered her paper grocery sack of chamomile and bread.

Ada clicked off the side table light, leaving the streetlamp to glow alone through the dingy sheers. She adjusted in the recliner, aligning her body with the lumps in the chair. She reminded herself to check the cabinets next door for teacups before locking the home up for the last time. She reached into her seersucker pocket and grasped the time-piece. She could feel the soft ticking of the second-hand keeping perfect rhythm with her grandfather clock.

And if she tried hard enough, with those keen ears of hers, she could hear the ticking of a thousand timepieces from one yard over and eight feet under. A single tear escaped from holding and traced the wrinkles down her cheek.

"Goodnight, Gil. Sleep tight."

About the Author

Beth enjoys chucking words into sentences then standing back to see what magic—or mayhem—falls out, crafting tales in mystery, sci-fi, fantasy, and general "slice of life" fiction. She couldn't accomplish this without the help of her tutu-clad Little Miss Muse and Trudi the Concrete Office Goose, who's partial to superhero capes.

Her stories have appeared in multiple publications, including Pulphouse Fiction Magazine and Ellery Queen Mystery Magazine, and in multiple fiction anthologies. She's received several Honorable Mentions from Writers of the Future. Her lighthearted blog peeks into the writing life as she pokes fun at herself and her circus of a life.

Follow the antics of Little Miss Muse and Trudi, read Beth's blog (she might have burned down her kitchen last week), and discover the stories at bapaul.com.